THIS BLOOMSBURY BOOK
BELONGS TO

....

For Becca and all the staff and children at York Rise Nursery,

with love and thanks — R.H.

For Val — S.H.

First published in Great Britain in 2007 by Bloomsbury Publishing Plc,
36 Soho Square, London, W1D 3QY

A CIP catalogue record of this book is available from the British Library

ISBN 978 0 7475 7303 6

Printed in Singapore

3 5 7 9 10 8 6 4 2

All papers used by Bloomsbury Publishing are natural, recyclable products made from wood grown in well-managed forests. The manufacturing processes conform to the environmental regulations of the country of origin.

Let's Take
Over The
Nursery!
RICHARD HAMILTON
PICTURES BY SUE HEAP
BLOOMSBURY
CHILDREN'S
BOOKS

Miss Tuck got stuck

in a climbing frame.

That was bad luck—

she won't do that again.

Because . . .

Oh, how we giggled
as Miss Tuck wriggled
and little Louis cried,
'Shut the teachers outside!

LET'S TAKE OVER THE NURSERY!'

Naughty Gemma locked the door.
'They can't come in here any more!'

'Do what you like,' cried Spike,
speeding around on a trike.

'Children, children,'
Said Miss Tuck.
'Stop this, please.
I'm really stuck.'

Water, water, everywhere!
In our shoes and in our hair!

Sticky glue,
gloopy glue.
Let us pour it
over you!

Paint the paper,
paint the floor,
paint the windows,
paint the door.

Paint your hands,
paint your face,
paint the paint
all over the place.

'Naughty children!' cried Miss Tuck.

(Then suddenly she had to duck.)

'Early lunch, I do decree!'
cried Louis from his balcony.
'Chocolate bread,' laughed Fred,
standing nearby on his head.

'I know,' cried cocky Clive.

'Let's push the cooker down the slide!'

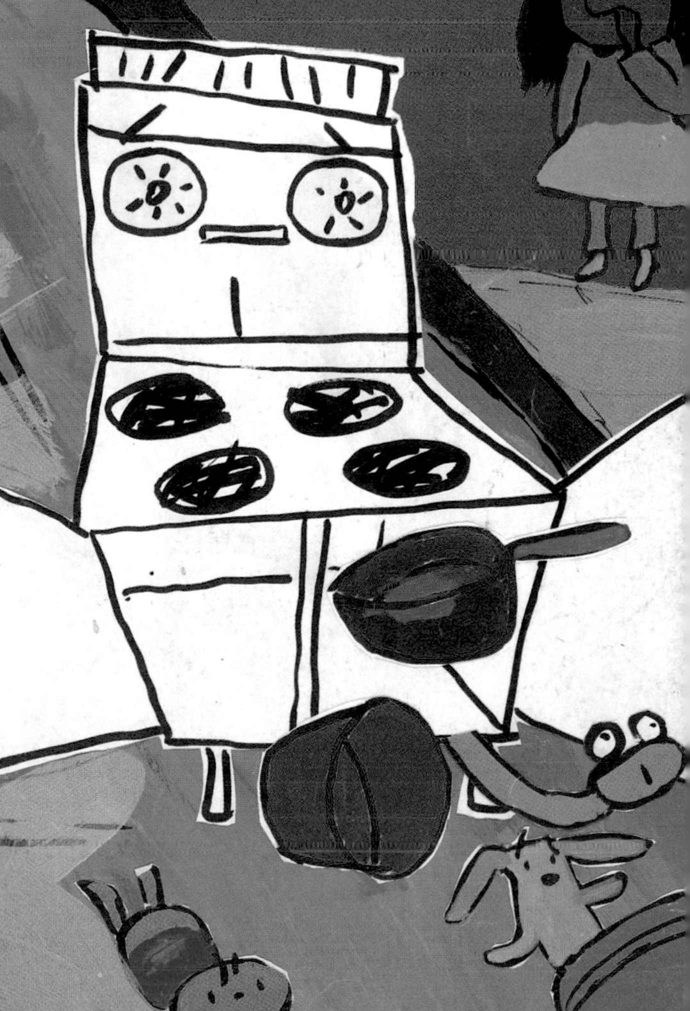

'Time to learn,'
said Beverley.
'A-B-C and 1-2-3.
Write your name,
sing a song.
Do a dance,
bang a gong.'

'Children, children, please be quiet.
This is a disgraceful riot!'

We were happy,
we were glad –
until things started turning bad.

Then Pip tripped Kip,
and hurt his lip.

And Milly sat on Tilly,

and Lily sat on Milly.

Then Molly took
Polly's dolly.

And Tim pinched Kim
till he cried . . .

And we all came running to Miss Tuck.

'Miss Tuck, Miss Tuck! Gemma poked me in the eye!'

'I feel sick!'

'I'm going to cry.'

'Annabel won't play with me.'
'Miss, I'm desperate for a wee!'
'Please Miss,' asked the tearful Rory. 'Who is going to read our story?'

Miss Tuck was stuck in the climbing frame.
'Come here,' she said, 'and play a little game...

Now stay calm, take my arm,
and pull as **hard** as you can.
And do not stop until I **pop**,
like popcorn in a pan!'

Hurray!

Up to Miss Tuck came Tilly and Milly,
and Pip and Kip and Molly and Polly,
and Kim and Tim and the tearful Rory.
And she gave us a hug and read us a story.

Enjoy more fantastic picture books from Bloomsbury Children's Books ...

A Pocketful of Kisses
Angela McAllister
Sue Hellard

A Big Kiss for Alice
Sally Grindley
Margaret Chamberlain

The Owl, the Aat, and the Roar
Tanya Linch

My First Day at Nursery
Becky Edwards
Anthony Flintoft